Mackenzie Bell

Spring's immortality, and other poems

with new prefatory note

Mackenzie Bell

Spring's immortality, and other poems
with new prefatory note

ISBN/EAN: 9783337374334

Printed in Europe, USA, Canada, Australia, Japan

Cover: Foto ©Andreas Hilbeck / pixelio.de

More available books at **www.hansebooks.com**

Spring's Immortality

AND

OTHER POEMS

By MACKENZIE BELL

AUTHOR OF "CHARLES WHITEHEAD: A FORGOTTEN GENIUS"

WITH NEW PREFATORY NOTE

SECOND EDITION

London

WARD, LOCK, AND BOWDEN, LIMITED

NEW YORK AND MELBOURNE

1895

To Edmund Clarence Stedman.

SEVERED from you by sundering seas I dwell—
   Never have clasped your hand, nor heard your
      voice—
   Never have seen your eyes make loving choice
Of mine to tell the truths words may not tell.

And yet I know you—oft in tranquil mood
   Your welcome songs—your wealth of critic
      lore—
   To me have brought a joy unfelt before,—
Or letters from you cheered my solitude.

January 19*th*, 1895.

Prefatory Note to Second Edition.

THE first edition of "Spring's Immortality and Other Poems" being exhausted, the volume has been entirely reset. In preparing a second edition for publication, I have made a few revisions, and, in deference to an opinion sometimes expressed, that the "Humorous Poems" were not in keeping with the other contents of the volume, have placed these in an Appendix.

One of my critics, to whose views I attach importance, has questioned the accuracy of my natural history, because in " Spring's Immortality " I say:

> " From many a stone the ouzels sing
> By yonder mossy stream."

—his contention being that the bird under such conditions merely says *Chit!* I venture to refer him to p. 71 of " British Birds in their Haunts," by the late Rev. C. A. Johns.   There that well-known naturalist, in the course of an interesting narrative about its habits, remarks that the dipper or water ouzel alights " on a wet mossy stone rising but a few inches above the water, where the stream runs swiftest and the spray sparkles brightest. But for the roar of the torrent you might hear his song, a low melodious strain."   Perhaps I ought to mention that I had not read the passage just quoted when I wrote "Spring's Immortality."

I have prefixed a poem addressed to my friend Mr. Edmund Clarence Stedman (to whom the book is dedicated), which originally appeared in " The Literary World."   It only remains for me to express my gratitude for the favourable reception which " Spring's Immortality and Other Poems " has received.

MACKENZIE BELL.

LONDON, *August,* 1895.

Contents.

Contents.

Contents. xiii

APPENDIX.

HUMOROUS POEMS.

Spring's Immortality.

THE buds awake at touch of Spring
    From Winter's joyless dream ;
From many a stone the ouzels sing
    By yonder mossy stream.

The cuckoo's voice, from copse and vale,
    Lingers, as if to meet
The music of the nightingale
    Across the rising wheat—

The bird whom ancient Solitude
    Hath kept for ever young,
Unaltered since in studious mood
    Calm Milton mused and sung.

Ah, strange it is, dear heart, to know
   Spring's gladsome mystery
Was sweet to lovers long ago—
   Most sweet to such as we—

That fresh new leaves and meadow flowers
   Bloomed when the south wind came;
While hands of Spring caressed the bowers,
   The throstle sang the same.

     *   *   *   *   *

Unchanged, unchanged the throstle's song,
   Unchanged Spring's answering breath,
Unchanged, though cruel Time was strong,
   And stilled our love in death.

The Lame Boy in the Woods.

EACH season hath its sadness, but for me
Summer hath most of all. I know not why,
But though its sylvan beauty soothes my soul
And brings sweet reveries—though the happy
     birds,
Discoursing music, stir my mind with dreams,
With melodies, with thoughts of deep delight;
Yet still there lurks within the Summer's heart
Or in mine own, a pain—a deep, wild pain—
Which, even amid still Autumn's ravages
I never feel, nor yet in Winter's storms.
Is it, I ask, that Summer's voiceless spell—
Her loveliness of copse and lea and flower
Is all too soon dissolved—that blossoms fade

When Summer's glory dies?

                    Ah, no; ah, no!
It is that Summer's mocking gladness lends
To loss a sharper sting when I recall
The joy of buoyant health and tireless limbs
Which others feel—alas! through all my life
A joy that knows not me.

Aspirations.

O FOR the poet's voice and song—
 Piercing, yet sweet and clear,
Rich as the cushat's note, yet strong
 To reach the great world's ear!

O for the visions that abide
 Within the poet's mind,
The thoughts which through his bosom glide
 Leaving strange joy behind!

O for the fruit—immortal fruit
 Soiled by no earthly leav'n,
Not fame alone, nor vain repute,
 But something caught from heav'n—

Assurance that my strain has cheered
 One soul, if only one,
And shed on the dark path it feared
 A passing glimpse of sun.

The Late Miss Christina Rossetti: an Interesting Forthcoming Volume.

Mr. Mackenzie Bell, who was a personal friend of the late Miss Christina Rossetti, and has a very intimate knowledge of her work, is engaged upon a volume of which she is the subject, and in which he will give not only some personal reminiscences, but much that is extremely interesting in regard to the extent to which her poetry was the result of her exceptionally striking personality. Upon the inner meaning of "Goblin Market," for instance, concerning which so many curious questions have been asked, Mr. Bell hopes to throw considerable light. His volume will also contain a series of chapters which will provide a detailed critical analysis of Miss Rossetti's fourteen books of poetry and prose. Mr. Bell holds that the development of her genius is illustrated in the volume of "Verses," printed privately by her grandfather in 1847, when she was sixteen years old, as well as in her contribution to *The Germ*, and to these considerable attention will be devoted. But while Mr. Bell's book will contain a great deal that is new and interesting to the literary public, his aim and hope is to make the volume sufficiently popular to serve, in the hands of those who are at present insufficiently acquainted with Miss Rossetti's work, as an introduction both to her Prose and her Poetry.

SONNETS.

Old Year Leaves.

Tossed by the storms of Autumn chill and drear,
   The leaves fall auburn-tinted, and the trees
   Stand reft and bare, yet on the silent leas
The leaves lie drifted still—while cold, austere,
Grim Winter waits—while early snowdrops cheer
   The woodland shadows—while the happy bees
   Are wakened by the balmy western breeze,
And birds and boughs proclaim that Spring is here.

So lost hopes severed by the stress of life
   Lie all unburied yet before our eyes,
      Though none but we regard their mute decay;
And ever amid this stir and moil and strife
   Fresh aims and growing purposes arise
    Above the faded hopes of yesterday.

In Memoriam, W. E. Forster.

(Obiit April 5th, 1886.)

O STALWART man and pure, whose earnest face
　　Mirrored thy fair-orbed soul, whose every deed
　　Made answer to thy word, who gav'st no heed
To selfish babble or the lust of place,
Who—grieving at thy country's perilous case
　　Grown dire by lack of knowledge—in her need
　　Cam'st with thy succour—thou whose civic creed,
Too wide for party, dealt with all the race.

A year hath passed since thou wast laid to rest,
Yet fragrant is thy memory; thy bequest
　　A work whose scope and grandeur Time shall
　　　　gauge.
Britain some day—her daughter-lands apart
No longer—will remember thee whose heart
　　Fired hers to win her world-wide heritage.

At the Grave of Dante Gabriel Rossetti.

April 9th, 1883.[1]

HERE of a truth the world's extremes are met :
  Amid the grey—the moss-grown tombs of those
  Who led long lives obscure till came the close
When, their calm days being done, their suns were
      set—
Here stands a grave, all monumentless yet,
  Wrapt like the others in a deep repose ;
  But while yon wakeful ocean ebbs and flows
It is a grave the world shall not forget—

This grave on which meek violets grow and thyme,
  Summer's fair heralds ; and a stranger now
    Pauses to see a poet's resting-place,
But one of those who will in many a clime
  On each return of this sad day avow
    Fond love's regret that ne'er they saw his face.

An Autumn Reminiscence.

A RADIANT garden rises on my view
Wherethrough the glowing hours the sunrays fall
Gently through hazel boughs; while brooklets
brawl
O'er beds where gleam the pebbles brown and blue.
Here, in that calm which never once they knew
On earth, dead heroes keep the slopes in thrall—
And russet ferns thereon, and dahlias tall,
And lilies white, and flowers of mingled hue.

Small wonder that these storied warrior forms
Should now in sculptured stone have rest, when I
Find here that Life's fierce conflicts seem to
cease—
Find respite here from all Life's rudest storms:—
Where still and silent 'neath a pale grey sky
Fair and contented Nature lies at peace.

Browning's Funeral.

I.

Venice, December 15th, 1889.

"The body of Robert Browning was conveyed to a
gondola which had the figure of an angel at the prow
and a lion at the stern, and was covered with flowers.
The relations and friends followed in gondolas across
the lagoon, in the light of the setting sun, to the ceme-
tery."

Now "past they glide," and bear the flower-
    wreathed bier
  Across the soundless waters, cold and grey,
Ere Night falls, sable-vestured and austere,
  And Day dies in one roseate flush away,
While they who follow, tearful, in the train
  See wonted sights with unfamiliar eyes;—
Like dreams, amid the fevered sleep of pain,
  Rich domes and frescoed palaces arise.

Yet haply, mixed with sorrow, dawns the thought
    How fit such obsequies for him whose pen
Hath given a wondrous poem,[2] passion-fraught,—
    Breathing of love and Venice,—unto men:
And so hath added to her deathless glory
A shining scroll of pure and ageless story.

II.

Westminster Abbey, December 31st, 1889.

The music of Croft and Purcell was used "as the Body
was brought into Church, and for the processional parts
of the burial service. This was followed by a 'medita-
tion,' composed for the service by Dr. Bridge, the words
from Elizabeth Barrett Browning's 'He giveth His belovèd Sleep.'"

CROFT'S solemn music swells; then comes at last
 The dim procession through the panelled choir;
And in the cloistral gloom, so still and vast,
 Many who loved him listen. Higher and higher
Rise Purcell's dirge-like tones, Grief's very soul,
 Yet soon " He giveth His belovèd Sleep "
Brings to our anguished hearts relief, control,
 Memories of stately Florence, and the deep

Love-sacrament which bound him to his spouse
  Changeless through changeful years. And· now
     in heaven
They meet in bliss—meet to renew their vows
  Beyond the soiling touch of earthly leaven.
While England, as 'tis right, in sacred trust
Keeps through the centuries his hallowed dust.

At Stratford-on-Avon.

SHAKESPEARE, thy legacy of peerless song
 Reveals mankind in every age and place,
In every joy, in every grief and wrong:
 'Tis England's legacy to all our race.
Little we know of all thine inner life—
 Little of all thy swift, thy wondrous years—
Years filled with toil—rich years whose days were
  rife
 With strains that bring us mirth, that bring us
 tears.
Little we know, and yet this much we know,
 Sense was thy guiding star—sense guided thee
To live in this thy Stratford long ago—
 To live content in calm simplicity;
Greatest of those who wrought with soul aflame
At honest daily work—then found it fame.

POEMS FOUNDED ON HISTORY.

The Taking of the Flag.

THE dawning light
Hath banished Night,
Breaking the ocean's sleep—
For all around
Is heard a sound
Of war upon the deep.

The Dutch and we
Are met at sea
On this blithe summer day,
To try at length
Our fighting strength
In battle's bloody fray.

See! on the right
Two ships in fight
In struggle long and hard,
And though so near,
They know not fear,
Close grappling yard to yard.

In very joy
An orphan boy
Speaks 'mid the battle's roar:
" Since morning's sun
The fight has run,—
When will it then be o'er?"

" 'Twill never lag
Till yon Dutch rag '
Down from the mast-head runs,
No other sign
Along our line
Can silence British guns."

" If thus it be,"
Then swift quoth he
With brightly flashing eye ;
" 'Twill soon be past,
Nor longer last,
Though if I fail, I die."

Hid by the cloak
Of sable smoke,
Full noiselessly he goes ;
Nor does he wait,
But springs elate
'Mid Britain's fiercest foes.

And up their mast
He clambers fast :
He grasps his precious prize :—
He knows no check—
He gains the deck,
With triumph in his eyes.

And through the roar
He bounds once more
To his appointed place;
Fearless, serene,
Is now his mien,
Fearless, serene his face.

Our men with glee
Shout "Victory!"
Waving the standard gay;
And from each gun
The Dutchmen run
In wonder and dismay.

And while their chief
Seeks, wild with grief,
To rally them in vain,
With one accord
Our sailors board,
And soon the vessel gain.

And of the youth
Who thus in truth
Had won a worthy name,
Men spoke aloud
In accents proud,
And world-wide was his fame.

The Keeping of the Vow.[4]

A.D. 1330.

KING ROBERT BRUCE is dying now,
  Heavily comes his breath,
And that last strife 'twixt death and life
  Will soon be won by death;

Around his couch the liegemen stand;
  They heave full many a sigh,
In dire dismay and grief are they
  To know their liege must die.

"Sir James of Douglas, come!" he cries,
  "Ever wert thou my friend,
And though we part, 'tis well thou art
  With me unto the end.

" When great my need I vowed to God
　　If He would grant to me
That war's surcease should bring us peace,
　　And Scotland should be free,

" His blessèd banner I would bear
　　To holy Palestine,
With arms to quell the Infidel :
　　Such was your King's design.

" Sore grieved am I that here I lie—
　　Death's hand upon my brow—
In vain, in vain, 'mid gnawing pain,
　　Do I recall my vow.

" Then promise me right faithfully,
　　When I am laid at rest,
That with my heart thou wilt depart
　　To do my last behest ! "

" My liege, I pledge my knightly word,
 Thy bidding shall be done,
The work is sad, yet am I glad
 Such favour to have won!

" Safe in my bosom shall thy trust
 Abide with me for ever,
Unless, perchance, in peril's hour,
 'Twere best that we should sever."

The king smiles faintly in reply—
 Then slowly droops his head,
And on the breast of him he loved
 Robert the Bruce lies dead.

In fit array at break of day
 Doth Douglas soon depart,
And in a casket carefully
 He keeps that Kingly Heart.

Crossing the main and sighting Spain,
   He joins the truceless war
Of Moor and Christian—that fierce strife
   Which rages as of yore; [5]

For straight he deems that here it seems
   His devoir first should be,
And with his host he swells the boast
   Of Spanish chivalry.

The armies twain on Tebas's plain
   Outspread—a goodly sight!
Eager they wait with hope elate,
   Impatient for the fight;

The summer sunbeams on the shields
   Of warriors brightly glancing,
Illume the mail of many a man
   And many a charger prancing,
And gallant crest that in the breeze
   Full gaily now is dancing;

Each Moslem there with scimitar,
    Upon his Arab horse,
Moves with a calm, a fearless mien,
    Unswerving in his course.

Lo here at length the stately strength
    The Cross and Crescent wield,
As deadly foes now darkly close
    Upon this fatal field.

The Spaniards' stroke hath broken through
    The dense opposing line !
Yet none the less both armies press
    Around their standard-sign,

While many a Paynim once so proud
    Lies lifeless on the plain,
And many a jennet of Castile
    Runs free with dangling rein.

First in the van the Douglas rides,
  With all his men-at-arms,—
A worthy company are they
  To front the Paynim swarms.

With bloody spur and loosened rein
  They break the stubborn foe,
So swift the chase they scarce can trace
  The course by which they go,

Till, looking back upon their track,
  The Paynim ranks they see
Have closed them in, 'mid dust and din
  With shout of wolfish glee.

" We find full late the danger great,"
  Sir Douglas cries, " return !
And charge the foe like Scots who know
  The rout at Bannockburn.

"Surely the men who conquered then
   Vain Edward's mighty host
Will never yield this sacred[5] field
   Nor let the base Moor boast."

So, boldly speaking, quick he turns—
   He gallops to the rear—
This dauntless quest through fierce unrest
   As gallant doth appear
As his who braves the foam-flaked waves
   To succour one most dear.

As Douglas passed the blows fell fast—
   Stern was the conflict wild,
With steeds and men, who ne'er again
   Would rise, the field was piled.

Yet, with his followers not a few,
   Now he has cleft his way
With flashing eye and flashing blade
   Straight through the grim array,

Once more he glances round, and sees,
   Still in the thickest fight,
Walter St. Clair, his well-beloved,
   A very valiant knight.

Full oft had they in tourney gay
   Their chargers deftly wheeled,
Full oft were nigh in days gone by
   On many a battle field,—

"Ride to the rescue!" Douglas shouts,
   "Ride on, and do not spare,
To save him from a woeful death
   Which of you will not dare!"

Urging his horse with headlong force,
   He seeks to render aid,
And many a tunic's fold is cleft
   By his resistless blade;

D

Yet is he left, of friends bereft,
　　Swart foemen all around,
Through the echoing strokes on helm and shield
　　Of help there comes no sound.

Now snatches he the jewelled casque
　　Where lies the Heart he loves,
('Tis strange to see how tenderly
　　His mailed hand o'er it moves),

And flings it forward, forward yet,
　　With this his battle cry,
"Press on, brave Heart, as thou wert wont:
　　I follow thee, or die!"

With lifted lance he makes advance
　　To where his treasure fell,
Each crash of blow—now fast, now slow—
　　Like a rude requiem knell,

And left alone, yet ne'er o'erthrown,
  He grapples with the foe,
Until a sword-thrust piercing him
  At last doth lay him low.

Then gallantly he struggles still,
  Half kneeling on the plain,
And there, o'erwhelmed by many a wound,
  The peerless knight is slain.

So died the chief, his life well lost
  In Scottish hero's work,
The stainless Douglas, he who sleeps
  In mossy Douglas kirk.

The Death of Captain Hunt.[7]

January 8th, 1761.

THE watch on board the *Unicorn*
　　Look out at dawn of light,
The sails are here, the sails at last!
　　The Frenchman heaves in sight.

And swiftly now the order comes
　　To give the Frenchman chase,
The Frenchman who is lost, we know,
　　If we can win the race.

Hurrah! the coward's flight is vain,
　　The ships are drawing nigh,
Each man prepares to win the fight—
　　To win the fight or die.

And soon the cannons' smoke and boom
    Are rolling all around,
Through two fierce hours of clangorous strife
    Is heard the deadly sound;

Wild scene of strange delirious joy,
    Yet desolating woe,
For now a shot our captain fells,
    And he is borne below.

Two seamen gently bear him down,
    And while the surgeon tries
To bind his wound, he looks on us
    With tender, pitying eyes.

The strife ne'er stays—the bearers bring
    Another blood-stained man.
" Surgeon," our captain says at once,
    " Go, save him if you can.

" My wound is mortal; thus for me
 Your care is all in vain,
Not so with him, then use your power
 To ease his heavier pain."

Soon ebbed our captain's tide of life—
 Short was the time for him—
Yet still his constant mind was clear
 Although his eyes grew dim.

And in a while his heart was glad
 For we had won the day,
His noble heart was satisfied—
 His spirit passed away.

The Loss of H.M.S. " Victoria."

June 22nd, 1893.

LET England mourn for these her gallant sons,
Who, seeing death was certain, yet remained
Steadfast to duty, all unconsciously
Grown to be heroes,—mourn for them whose souls,
Fired with immortal courage, conquered fear.
Let England grieve with them who, silent, weep
A loss irreparable with bitter tears.
Let England grieve for him who, though he erred
Soon felt perchance, in feeling he had erred,
An agony more great than death itself.

    *   *   *   *   *

Let England still rejoice, for now she knows,
Though Time and Science change the face of war,
The stuff of English hearts they cannot change.

PICTURES OF TRAVEL.

Palms by Moonlight at Alicante.

Palms by moonlight! waving palms,
    How the thought of you embalms
In memory still the spot whereon I saw you last!
    Softly, wonderfully clear
    On that night did you appear
Whose blissful hours, swift-winged, too soon, too
      soon, were past.

    Here the eye could range at will,
    And of beauty take its fill,
Beauty so rare it soothed as soothes a heav'n-sent
      dream—
    Or a mellow Eastern tale
    Where the genii ride the gale
And glide among such trees on many a moonlight
      gleam.

For the strange ethereal sight
Thrilled me with a new delight,
While still the full-orbed moon o'er leaf o'er
    feathery bough
From a sky of purest blue
Silver glory gently threw.
Then rapturous visions came I know not whence
    or how—

Visions, sweet and kind, that stole
Through my hush'd and happy soul
To strive against their power had been a vain
    endeavour,
And, with ravished eye and heart,
Wished I never to depart,
Looking, I longed to live, and see these sights for
    ever.

João to Constança.

(A Lesté [8] sunrise in Madeira.)

YONDER flush across the sea
Brings the morning back to me
When you seemed to lend the light
That dispersed the lingering night;
When I heard your step, and knew
Joy of joy! 'twas surely you;
When I turned and saw your face,
Saw you glide with girlish grace;
Though before my heart was moved,
Then it was that first I loved.

Rosy cloudlets, lately dun,
Seemed as now to hide the sun;

Other cloudlets seemed to stand
Ready waiting his command.
Brighter, brighter grew the group,
Every tint was in the troop,
Red, and blue, and rich maroon,
Fleecy white appearing soon,
As at length we plighted troth,
Hallowed moments for us both.

O'er the peaks the vapoury shrouds
Shifted with the shifting clouds;
Faintly purpled clouds were spread
O'er the peaceful ocean's bed;
Clouds empurpled now, and grand,
Cast a halo o'er the land.
Every bird and opening flower
Felt the gladness of the hour,
As the gentle landward breeze
Stirred the tall banana-trees.

You remember how the day,

While dawn's freshness wore away,

Took a dimmer purple hue

As the clouds were changed anew,

You remember how we walked,

You remember how we talked,

How, beneath this trellised vine,

Oft you told me you were mine,

Each remembrance makes more clear

All the debt I owe you, dear.

Francisca to Jaspear:

A Madeiran Idyl.

THE rich—the rich alone—may dream of death
As solace for their sorrow, not the poor.
Whate'er their grief, the poor have work to do
If they would not behold their dear ones starve.
Now were *I* dead there's none to pluck the fruit
And sort it on our stall o' market days,
Mother is ill, and through the scorching hours
Father is busy 'mid the sugar-canes.

It seems but yesterday since you and I,
Happy with thoughts of coming happiness,
Lived in the future, for the pleasant years
Stretched all before us, fraught with all the joy

That only love which changes not can give.

Never shall I forget how once we sat

Here where the orange-trees yield grateful shade,

As with fond eyes of truth you told to me

Once and again the sweet familiar tale

That ever to a maiden's heart is new.

Far, far beneath me, shimmering in the sun,

Were palms with shapely branches, outlined now

More clearly by the strong light pouring down,

And nearer, on the left, an avenue

Of red and white camellias full in flower

Formed one long vista filled with varying hues,

While countless clustering vines and citron trees

Gleamed in a rare, a radiant mingled glow

Of gorgeous colour.   The banana-trees,

Each with its fragrant load of luscious fruit,

The graceful guavas with their light-green leaves,

The loquats with their deeper verdant tints,

E

The stately yam-trees with their blossoms white,
Stood forth in all their loveliness together.

Delightful was it, when the sun declined,
To loiter with you as the breath of night
Conquered the sultry ardour of the day;
To see the moon rise over silent seas;
To see the summer heavens, now decked with stars,
Vie with the shafts of distance-mellowed light
From many a cottage on the lone crag-sides
In making a rich girdle round the bay;
To hear the soft *machéte*⁹ play some air
Of gayest sound, perhaps a mazy dance.

Alas! alas for me, such hours of bliss
Can nevermore return, for you are dead.
Good were it if I lay where you are laid
In that fair spot where one may hear the waves
Break idly on the shingle beach below
In noontide heat when scarce a lizard stirs;

Where scented roses cling around the tombs
Still blooming on throughout the sunny year.

    *   *   *   *   *

Yes, mother, I am coming, you must look
At these my oranges, fresh plucked and ripe,
And at my custard apples, they will be
The finest in the market-place to-day.

Christmas in the Summer Sunshine.

(Funchal, Madeira.)

CHRISTMAS in the summer sunshine! O how
wonderful it seems,—
Dowered with gladness are its moments, realizing
poet-dreams,
While its moments hasten from me, how I wish
they came to stay,—
How I wish their guileless pleasure nevermore
might pass away.

Softly play around my forehead breathings of the
seaward breeze,
As it stirs the swaying branches of the palms and
orange-trees,—

As it stirs the cactus growing on the gaunt uprising
    cliffs
Hanging o'er the gleaming ocean dotted with the
    fishing skiffs.

Nature here with slightest tendance grants her
    gifts of loveliest hue—
Gives among the vine-clad ridges wild-flowers
    purple, golden, blue,—
Here azaleas, rich gardenias ope their blossoms to
    the air,
With the rose and trained geranium—whose wild
    types are also fair.

Pure and calm the moonlight radiance for the
    people as they pass
On the eve of merry Christmas to and from the
    midnight mass;
While the jocund serenaders through the balmy
    hours of night

By their songs and sprightly music often bring a
brief delight.

Christmas in the summer sunshine! neither frost
nor snow are here,
Buoyant health can welcome winter but it fills the
sick with fear—
Here the sick with friends around them spend a
cheerful Christmas day,
Thinking of but seldom pining for a chill home
far away.

Verses

On a vase filled with sub-tropical flowers grown in
the open air at Madeira, in December.

Most beauteous flowers!
Come ye to tell of summer hours,
Of balmy breezes—lengthened days,
 Of warblers' blithesome lays?

 Thus come ye not,
For not in summer lies your lot,
No lengthened days attend your birth
 Nor songsters' vocal mirth.

Yet gentle gales
Are near, and sunshine still prevails,
As in frail loveliness ye lie
   Too soon, alas! to die.

Ah fair, how fair,
Here Nature working everywhere,—
If winter thus it makes to me,
   What must the spring-time be!

And yet, although
Each plant delights in southern glow,
Upon no zephyr is there spent
   One breath of subtle scent.

'Tis England's flowers—
The lily and rose of English bowers—
Retain the perfume and the glow:
   These blossoms only blow.

'Tis England's spring
Whose every floweret seems to bring
New sweets to blend with every breeze
   Among the budding trees.

   Yet 'tis a power,
This glory of each plant and flower,
To make the poet's heart rejoice
   And sing with gladsome voice.

   The poet feels—
Yet rarely even he reveals—
The restful store of blissful thought
   Such flowers to him have brought.

On the Road to Camara de Lobos, Madeira.

January, 18—.

THE sun that is setting afar in the west
In raiment of glory goes down to his rest,
And, like a young maiden who wishes good-bye
To the lover when leaving her, blushes the sky;
How fair is the picture as now in the west
In raiment of glory the sun goes to rest.

The clouds in apparel of sunset appear,
Apparel of beauty while Evening draws near,
While calmly they watch o'er the sleep of the sea
Unstirred by the breezes.   How wondrous to me
Is the peace of the picture, as now in the west
In raiment of glory the sun goes to rest.

How peerless and perfect God's painting appears,
His delicate work never fades with the years;
His painting now quiet, now wild beyond speech,
Man only can copy, man never can reach
In grandeur. So thought I, as now in the west
In raiment of glory the sun goes to rest.

Sunday Morning off Mazagan, Morocco.

A MAGIC city Fancy-dight,
Thou seem'st this tranquil Sabbath day,
   Strange town all glittering, treeless, white,
Begirt with sand and seething spray—

   Lit by the sun whose rays reveal
Each flat-roofed Orient dwelling-place,—
   Each stately mosque, each well whose wheel
A camel turns with tireless pace.

   Dark Moors in their fantastic dress,
In haste to reach us, leave the shore,—
   They make the distance less and less,
So strong the stroke of each long oar.

Now they have reached us and with pride
Disdain the aid the steps afford,
 Bare feet from heel-less slippers glide,
And, cat-like, quick they spring on board.

 All speak at once, with gestures quaint,
And few but in an unknown tongue,
 Those in the boats take up the plaint,
And on the deck still more have sprung.

 A single ship is in the bay
Besides our own,—no others ride
 At anchor. And she goes her way—
But not until to-morrow's tide.

 And from her mizen-mast there floats—
Dear sight to every British heart—
 That flag whose mingled hue denotes
A union naught should ever part.

A welcome standard ! 'tis a sign—
A welcome sign—that some are here
Who worship at a common shrine,
Who pray like me—like me revere.

On Looking up the Vale of Cauterets, Hautes Pyrénées, by Night.

Though night is here,
  In outline soft I see
A vista through the gloom, where, mirrored clear,
  Gleam rock and peak and tree.

  The mountain forms
  In solemn grandeur rise,
Each summit still the strength of countless storms
  For countless years defies.

  The dark-green pines
  Clothe all the slopes around—

How lone these slopes on which each cold star
    shines!
  Nor doth a single sound

    Invade the calm,—
  Or by its presence change
The sense of vastness, soothing like a balm,
  From heaven so new and strange.

The Southern Night.

(The Valley of the Gave de Pau.)

Ah! lovelier comes the southern night
  Than night of northern skies,
Where tedious twilight mocks the flight
  Of day that slowly dies—
Here placid Evening's starry veil
  O'er all is swiftly cast—
Here peace seems wafted on the gale—
  And care awhile is past.

Iu southern summer's mellow night
  How sweet it is to stray
'Mid fairest scenes which soft moonlight
  Make fairer far than day!

F

How fair the widely stretching woods
   That gird the spacious plain,
While watchful Silence, queen-like, broods
   O'er them in sombre reign—
How fair the river's crystal thread,
   Seen faintly from afar,
As silvery starlight now is shed
   From many a tranquil star.

In southern summer's mellow night
   How sweet it is to stray
'Mid fairest scenes which soft moonlight
   Make fairer far than day !

How fair the crested mountains lie,
   Distant, yet wondrous clear,
Their snow-capt peaks against the sky
   Uprising tier on tier ;—
How fair the sleeping landscape seems,
   While here and there are heard

Sounds bringing Music's richest dreams
  Or laughter-laden word.

In southern summer's mellow night
  How sweet it is to stray
'Mid fairest scenes which soft moonlight
  Make fairer far than day !

Lines:

Suggested by seeing, at the summit of the Simplon
Pass, a stone, fragment of some rude ancient
carving, brought perhaps from a neighbouring
valley for road-making purposes. The stone had
lain doubtless for a long time near the spot where
I saw it.

How strange perchance have been, quaint carven
  stone,
  Your harsh vicissitudes, how came you here?
Change spares not even you, though you have
  known
  No soul-distress, nor Sorrow's blinding tear,
  Nor deep unutterable heart-wrought fear.

Did you of some calm shrine once form a part
  Where vesper hymns arose at close of day,
Where lovers true were linkèd heart to heart,
  And humble villagers approached to pray,
  Then, rising, went refreshed upon their way ?

And did fierce war destroy your place of peace
  When some forgotten skirmish happened there
Ere yet the Austrian yoke was made to cease
  By famed Marengo ? [10] Bullets did not spare
  The lowly church, and fire soon laid it bare.

Maybe, when fickle Time had brought neglect,
  When reverence was a thing of long ago,
When none in all the hamlet had respect
  For its old ruined fane, they came to throw
  Its remnants thus away, and used you so.

Near you, must oft have wandered weary men
  'Mid dire storm-battles fought on wintry
    nights ;—

Near you, perchance, have happened now and then
　　More wondrous deeds, more awe-inspiring sights
　　Than sages know in whom the world delights.

What mighty tempests must have passed you by
　　When 'mid the riven mountains thunder pealed,
And storm-clouds came apace athwart the sky
　　In mad career, while Nature half revealed
　　The grandeur of the tumult, half concealed

Its majesty and power.　The silent snows
　　Must oft have lain upon you, when the hands
Of Winter framed his lofty couch, and chose
　　His glacier lairs—when all the higher lands
　　Loomed ghastly, shuddering at his dread com-
　　　mands

In solemn midnight hours when callous stars
　　Shine down on snow-drifts, on the glaciers lone,
And on snow-laden pines: when nothing mars

That spectacle to human eyes scarce known,
Where Nature rears 'mid rocks her frost-bound
  throne.

Yet are you broken now to make a road—
  Fallen from your pristine state, and haply too
You will be worthless in your chill abode,
  And shrink from man's unfeeling, heedless view
  In your small nook, ignoble, poor, and new.

In the New Forest.

Most clear! most fair!
The swelling woodland lies,
Stretching in leafy glory everywhere
Before my wondering eyes.

Here mighty oaks,
Stalwart, and vast, and strong,
A thousand years have faced the tempest's strokes—
Have been the home of song.

Here wave the boughs
Of tall and sombre pines,
Here stands "the temple of beeches," made for
vows
Of love when softly shines

The summer moon.
Here tremulous branches sway
Of sun-lit birches,—on the sward at noon
Their shadows seem at play.

I linger still
In this sweet solitude,
Wishing my care-sick mind could taste at will
The healing sylvan mood.

RELIGIOUS POEMS.

God's Peace.

" The peace of God which passeth all understanding."
Phil. iv. 7.

How oft amid the griefs of life—
    Perplexed, misjudged, distressed—
O God, I waver in the strife,
    And long and cry for rest.
How oft I feel—so great my need,
    My courage so outworn—
As though my griefs were now indeed
    Greater than could be borne.

Yet oft will come in times like these—
    Come like a gracious balm—
A sense of peace, of joy, of ease,
    A sense of heaven's own calm.

Ah! then my heart would fain express
    What I have felt before—
'Tis not I feel my griefs are less—
    I feel Thy love is more.

And some are here, O God, to-day,
    Here with their voiceless grief,
O give the aid for which they pray,
    O give such sweet relief,
O give Thy peace, Thy calm, Thy joy,
    Here as they humbly bow—
Such gifts nor Time nor Change destroy,
    Give them, and give them *now*.

A Rallying Song.

Sometimes trustful, often fearful,
  In this world of shifting wrong;
Sometimes joyful, often tearful,
  Still be this our rallying song—
      Aye, in sadness
      And in gladness,
  Nobly act, for God is strong.

When, oppressed by deep soul-sorrow,
  Life beneath the darkest skies
Seems so drear that no to-morrow
  Holds a threat of worse surprise—
      In such sadness
      As in gladness
  Nobly act, for God is wise.

When our souls are tried, and tempted
Some ignoble end to buy,
From the coward's bonds exempted,
Let us resolutely cry—
Evil sow not,
That it grow not,
Nobly act, for God is nigh.

Morning Thoughts.

SWEET-VOICED songsters softly singing
  Tell me of a day begun,
Its appointed portion bringing
  Of the duty to be done.

Last day's deeds are gone for ever,—
  Seems it not most passing strange
Their results remain, and never
  Can be touched by time or change?

Like a child, his pebble throwing
  From the streamlet's sedgy marge,
Marking not the ripples growing
  Though they one by one enlarge—

G

So, with influence still increasing,
  Widening o'er Life's mystic sea,
Man deals out his actions,—ceasing
  Only with Eternity.

Many yesterday, unthinking,
  Chose the road which leads to night,—
While a few, with souls unshrinking,
  Chose the pathway of the light.

Thus I muse with deep emotion
  Whilst the moments melt away—
Muse upon the boundless ocean
  Of the issues of *to-day*.

A Song of Comfort.

Not always have we sorrow, there are seasons
  When buoyant joy dispels all dreams of ruth—
Times when our thoughts of sorrow seem but
    treasons
    To king-like Truth.

Not always are we vext by cares and troubles,—
  Often the griefs of life appear no more—
Vanished, as on a lake the rain-drop bubbles,
    When showers are o'er.

Not always feel we that our hopes are blighted;
  A glad fruition will they often gain,
When we perceive the good are aye requited
    Who conquer pain.

Not always should we grieve, each tribulation
   Is sent to purify—to raise the soul,
To fit it for its glorious destination—
   A heavenly goal.

The Balance of Life.

'Tis false to say the world, though sad,
   Hath no redeeming feature,
'Tis false to say the world, though glad.
   Can hold no hopeless creature.

The darkest life has oft a ray
   Of sunshine on the morrow,
The brightest life has many a day
   Whose hours are filled with sorrow.

No life with ceaseless grief is fraught,
   None with all bliss and beauty,
By varied teaching are we taught
   The way to walk in duty.

If happy be our earthly lot,
    And free of Sorrow's burden,
Greater the need to linger not;—
    Our work shall have its guerdon:

Yet richer guerdon comes to those
    Whom heav'n hath not exempted
From pain, who quell the self-same foes
    Although more sorely tempted.

Each grief that sweeps across the heart,
    If sinless be its sadness,
In Life's long lesson bears a part
    And yields us future gladness.

" Lord, Teach us to Pray."

Luke xi. 1.

A DARK enigma is our life
　　Without Thy guiding ray ;
Then calm, O Christ, its sordid strife
　　By teaching us to pray.
Prayer is Heaven's torch when doubts and fears
　　With darkness cloud our way,—
Its holy radiance guides and cheers,—
　　What peace it brings to pray !

Oft lies our path through pain and woe
　　While in Earth's night we dwell,
Yet prayer is still a light to show
　　That aye Thou leadest well ;

So when Life's mysteries distress,
    And Sorrow bars our way,
We plead that Thou wouldst make it less
    By teaching us to pray.

Holy Quietude.

Spirit of holy quietude,
   For thee my soul is sighing—
For thee in many a mournful mood
   My soul is blindly crying—
But still a voice comes softly clear,
"That spirit seldom cometh here."

Spirit of holy quietude,
   While, weary, I am breasting
Life's waves, bring with thee all things good—
   Deep peace, and joy, and resting:—
Yet still the voice—"No, never here
Doth she thy soul would find appear."

Spirit of holy quietude,
    Grant me a single token—
Show me that Life's long conflict rude
    By gleams of peace is broken;
But the voice whispers in mine ear,
" That spirit never dwelleth here."

Spirit of holy quietude,
    Mine earthly course is ending,
Now let thy peace within me brood,
    Sin's strongest fetters rending;
" In heaven," the voice says at my side—
" In heaven alone doth she abide."

LYRICS AND MISCELLANEOUS
POEMS.

The Unfulfilled Ideal.

WHEN youthful Summer decks the sward
  With flowers on plain and hill,
And Nature wins her meet reward
  For working Winter's will,
Even then Life's music lacks a chord:
  Something wanted still!

In Autumn, when each searing leaf
  With gentle sorrow fraught,
And every garnered golden sheaf
  Yield fruit for mingled thought :—
We feel a void—there comes a grief—
  Something vaguely sought!

When Winter lays an icy hand
   Where Spring had kissed the ground,
And stiff and stark is all the land
   Where Summer erst was crowned:—
We feel but do not understand:
   Something still unfound!

When Spring returns with radiant grace
   To fill the earth with song,
And gladness smiles in every place,
   And love and life are strong,
Still comes the want we cannot trace:
   Something wanted long!

The Child Cowper at Berkhampstead.

"Where the gard'ner Robin, day by day,
Drew me to school along the public way."
          COWPER, *My Mother's Picture.*

BRIGHT beams of sunshine lit the lawn,
And all the landscape seemed as drawn
  From some enchanter's treasure ;—
The birds were singing loud and clear,
But most perchance he loved to hear
  The blackbird's cheery measure.

And while he loiter'd 'neath the trees
Soft scents were wafted by the breeze
  That blew across the hay-field

Where village children then resorted,
And as among the swaths they sported
   Transformed it to a play-field.

Did these dear visions fade away?
They did—and for their death that day
   He felt a throb of sorrow;
But gladness came in sorrow's place
When Hope said with her smiling face,
   " 'Twill live again to-morrow."

In Ellington Copse.

How lovely are these woodland ways
   Clad in their summer dress,
Where come not din and smoke to mar
   Their evening loveliness;

Where wild-rose and convolvulus
   Are wov'n in every hedge,
And buttercups and foxgloves glow
   By this clear brooklet's edge;

Where breezes waft their balmiest scents
   Adown the silent wood,
And scarce a songster sings to break
   The hush of solitude;

H

Where shadows creep across my path
    And softly dies the day—
And Summer's beauty holds the world
    Within her gracious sway.

This evening every wild-flower here
    More deeply stirs my heart
Than alien flowers or prodigies
    Of man's botanic art;

This sweet-brier bough, that meekly sends
    Its perfume on the air,
I would not give for any flower
    The gardener deems most fair;

I leave the rich their bowers of art
    Wreathed with the rarest flowers,
Enough for me these woodland ways
    In Summer's twilight hours.

A Song of Early Summer.

Sweet is the time when tender leaves
   Burst forth in all their perfect grace,
When swallows twitter from the eaves,
   And Spring to Summer yields her place;

When red and white the chestnut shows,
   When fragrance from the hawthorn spreads,
When fair the blue wistaria blows,
   And iris lilies lift their heads.

Yet soon the chestnut petals fade,
   Wistaria blooms droop one by one,
Soon sigh the leaves for welcome shade,
   Then fall with dews at set of sun.

Not so the spring-time of the heart,
    That knows nor change nor swift decay,
The spring-time of our nobler part
    Shall never fade or pass away.

The Heart's Summer.

Sweet is the noon of a summer day
　When, through the woodlands coming,
The village sounds seem far away
　And drowsy bees are humming.

Sweet are the hours of a summer night
　When kindly dews are falling,
And thoughts that come with the fading light
　Are soothing, or enthralling.

Sweet are the tones of a friendly voice
　When all seems gone but sorrow,
Bidding the heart once more rejoice,
　For peace may come to-morrow.

Sweet is the sound of the world's applause
When fame at last hath found us,
And (wage for toil in a righteous cause)
Flings victory's wreath around us.

But sweeter far is a heart at rest,
A heart unsoured by sadness—
Which throbs within a blissful breast
With a God-imparted gladness.

The Autumn is Dying.

THE autumn is dying,
　　And leaves that are still,
Grief's tokens, are lying
　　On plain and on hill;
My garden of pleasure
　　Lies withered and bare,
Oh the pitiless measure
　　Of ruin wrought there.

In a hedgerow wind-shaken
　　To wildest unrest,
Forlorn and forsaken
　　I see a bird's nest,

Its soft down decaying,
　　Its fledglings all flown,
Naught save the shell staying
　　Deserted and lone.

Then the thought rises, cleaving
　　The depths of my mind,
Soon we too shall be leaving
　　Our loved homes behind,
Soon the grave will enclose us—
　　Life's pilgrimage o'er—
" And the place that now knows us
　　Shall know us no more."

December Daisies and December Days.

Ah, how the sight of these untimely flowers
Brings dear remembrances of summer hours,
When the full heart in buoyant mood was filled
With happiness—when the swift moments thrilled
The soul with subtle thoughts no words express.

Kind halcyon moments! How they soothe and
    bless
And beautify my sordid life. And here,
When this December day is stir-less, clear
At its brief twilight—when there shines afar
From out a cloudless heav'n yon evening star—
When southern breezes blow, nor storm nor rain
Disturb,—I dream 'tis summer come again.

The Poet's Inspiration.

True inspiration ever seems
   A joy and yet a pain,
To light the poet's lofty dreams,
   To purify his strain.

Its presence glorifies the line
   Whose rhythmic measure halts,
Makes hackneyed thoughts seem half divine,
   Till few perceive such faults.

And thus, although we sometimes find
   Imperfect chords like these
In songs of many a master-mind,
   How seldom they displease:

But when its presence is not felt,
   Though smooth the verses roll—
Though cadences in sweetness melt—
   They cannot stir the soul.

A Memory and a Presence.

WHEN clasping in mine own the hand
  Of him I loved the best,
Whose converse cheered, as sight of land
  Cheers mariners distressed,
How once I loved the darkening hour
  Of Summer's happy day,
As gently from each leaf and flower
  The daylight passed away.

For he had learnt to bear his part
  In Earth's unending strife,
To labour with unflinching heart
  Amid the ills of life—

To feel adversity and pain,
  Hopes blighted, bitter wrong,
And yet, ere long, to find again
  God's peace which makes men strong.

So would he talk of bygone years
  In that hush'd eventide,
Of former hopes, delights, and fears,
  Of early friends who died,
And wisely would my future trace,
  Then leaving things of Time,
In raptured tones, with upturned face,
  Would speak of themes sublime.

He had that wordless eloquence,
  That strange, that wondrous power,
Which sways the soul with force intense
  In calm of such an hour;

And walking where the shadows steal
 Across the garden here,
Alone with memory still I feel
 His spirit ever near.

" While the Sunset, slowly Dying."

WHILE the sunset, slowly dying,
　　Sheds a light o'er sea and strand,
And the night-chilled breeze is sighing
　　As the darkness wraps the land—
Come, with influence strong yet tender,
　　Mingled thoughts of vanished years,
Waking soul-thrills that can render
　　Sometimes joy and sometimes tears.
All the past, returning, seems
Present with its living dreams.

When the kindly summer's glory
　　Filled the earth with myriad charms,
First I breathed a lover's story—
　　First I felt true love's alarms—

First I pleaded with a maiden,
　　Hazel-eyed, and pure, and fair
As that eve whose gales love-laden
　　Wantoned with her auburn hair.
All the past, returning, seems
Present with its living dreams.

Now to me how swiftly thronging
　　Come the visions of the past—
Treasured past to me belonging—
　　Span of bliss too deep to last:
Still do I remember clearly
　　What I asked in trembling tone,
And her words, " I love you dearly,
　　Yours I am, and yours alone."
All the past, returning, seems
Present with its living dreams.

We were " wedded, happy-hearted,"
　　And our future path seemed bright,

Who could tell we should be parted,
　　Love's glad sun obscured in night?
Yet one eve, when softly sighing
　　Summer breezes lulled the rose,
I beheld her, fainting, dying,
　　I beheld her dim eyes close.
Ah, how living, fraught with woe,
Rise the sights of long ago!

＊　　＊　　＊　　＊　　＊

Yet amid my sore dejection
　　Comes the comfort ever new—
Comes the balm, the sweet reflection,
　　To each other we were true.
For some end God sendeth sorrow,
　　When that end is gained at last,
In the radiant heavenly morrow
　　We shall meet—all sorrow past.
There, no longer fraught with woe,
Rise the days of long ago.

I

The Bride's Song.

A FEW days more, a few days more,
  And all the world will change!
For I shall enter through Love's door
  To something sweet yet strange—
To that new home where comes no fear
  Unshared by him I love—
And I shall always, always hear
  His voice where'er I rove.

Ah then, ah then, my duty lies
  With him, and him alone,
Less duty than delight, surprise,
  To me before unknown—

Delight that I am ever nigh
　To do each fond behest,
Surprise that I, and only I,
　Can make his life more blest.

.

Oft does he praise my sunny hair,
　The bloom upon my cheeks—
Would that I were indeed so fair
　When thus my dear one speaks.
I feel myself unworthy, yet
　He takes me for his wife,
But I will yield—to pay my debt—
　The service of my life.

The Hawthorn Spray.

HAPPY, with that strange happiness
  Which Spring spreads o'er the land,
I see a girl, I see a boy,
  They are walking hand in hand.
I hear them as they gaily talk,
  They heed no future care,
He plucks a flushing hawthorn spray
  To deck her fairer hair.

" And let this be a token now,"
  The merry boy exclaims,
" That, some time in the coming years,
  We two may link our names.

The may-buds are a symbol meet
   Of this our treaty pure,
So may our compact bring us joy
   And evermore endure."

    *   *   *   *   *

These two—though many years have fled—
   Fled like a dream away,
Are still as true of heart as on
   That unforgotten day.
And so together oft again
   Amid the spring-tide's glow
They walk, remembering thankfully
   Their love-pledge long ago.

The Puritan's Farewell to his Betrothed, 1642.

SHE—

WHEN Love arose and taught my heart
　To hold thee first and chief,
I never dreamed that we should part
　In pain beyond belief,
Then wherefore bring this aching woe
　To me, to thee, to all,
E'en though harsh Duty bids thee go
　To obey thy faction's call?

HE—

Nay, speak not so; that sigh, that look,
　Wound worse than blades of steel,

Yet what were I if I forsook,
  Because of thine appeal,
No "faction" but God's righteous cause,
  No struggle of greed and shame—
One stern last stand for Right and laws
  That win His high acclaim?

Truth, Justice, Conscience plead with me,
  Then wouldst thou have me, dear,
For calm and ease and joy with thee
  To yield to craven fear—
To prove a recreant from the right—
  A coward sore afraid—
A traitor in the coming fight
  Where England needs mine aid?

Thou murmur'st, "We shall meet no more:"
  I know, I know thy pain,
Our life is brief, but when 'tis o'er
  True lovers live again—

They live again in that fair land
    Where comes nor strife nor sword—
Where Truth and Joy go hand in hand—
    And Love hath Faith's reward.

There, where each feeling stands confessed,
    Wilt thou know all my sorrow—
Wilt know what pangs have rent my breast
    Ere leaving thee to-morrow.
Lo, hearken to the distant chime,
    To us a knell of sadness,
Then let us spend our span of time
    In peace more deep than gladness.

SHE—

The weakness goes: oh, heed it not!
    My fears have done thee wrong;
My pain is but my woman's lot,
    And Love shall make me strong :—

In these brave arms I will be brave,
    And while thou still art here,
To God will lift my soul, and crave
    The peace which casts out fear.

Passion's Slave.

BLIND passion ever showed its maddening power
Enthroned within him—a sin-garnered dower
Of quenchless loves and longings. That fierce
    storm
Which breaks the boughs of Life, where sheltered
    warm
Repose, like unfledged nestlings, Life's chief joys,
Swept o'er his soul—the wave that swift destroys
Man's store of peace. What years of labour cost
He by one fatal step for ever lost.

Two Lives.

A COTTAGE home : a peaceful place
Where Sorrow hides her pallid face ;
Husband and wife, a happy pair,
Who thankfully Life's blessings share ;
And living far from towns' turmoil,
They simply crave a " leave to toil ! "

*　　　*　　　*　　　*　　　*

A workhouse full of dreary din,
Full of the signs of want and sin.
A man and woman sinking fast,
Sinking, yet conscious to the last,
Their senses steeped in wrathful woe
None but the frugal poor can know

When first, despite their care, is spent
Their all through sickness and the rent;
When first, despite their abject grief,
No kindly landlord grants relief;
When first, despite their abject gloom,
His agent comes—decrees their doom;
When first within the workhouse gate
Silent they stand, how desolate!
When first they feel, with sorrow bowed,
The loneliness amid a crowd—
When first they feel in their distress
That is the deepest loneliness;
When first they feel they near their end,
Yet by their bed no former friend;
When now, despite their struggles—struggles
　　　long and brave—
Their death but fills—but helps to fill—a
　　　pauper's grave.

To Sir Walter Scott.

(Written after reading his "Journal.")

Poet, 'twas no strange sun that shone on thee
Through thy pure life so crowned with dignity,
No sun with light now clouded, now intense,
But aye the unclouded sun of common sense.

Solitude.

AMID the throng
Which, restless, moves along
With hurrying footsteps o'er the earth,
But few their noblest thoughts have known,
Seldom save when alone
Come thoughts of worth.

It needs the balm
Of soul-restoring calm
To purge the mind of Life's alloy;
Thus yielding back Man's highest power,
His blessèd pristine dower
Of peace and joy.

And thus do men
With new and eager ken
Taste those rich joys that only live
In solitude—joys which uplift
Their souls to truth—best gift
That Life can give.

APPENDIX.

HUMOROUS POEMS.

Moonlight on the Tagus.

THE moon shines o'er the Tagus.   Now a flood
Of soft-spun sparkling radiance clothes the scene
With dazzling splendour, save where shadows lie
Upon the river's bosom, sheltering there
The coward Darkness, here dethroned awhile,
By the moon's great though seeming gentle might.
Ah me, how beautiful! Deep azure sky,
Deep azure sea, and steadfast-beaming stars,—
A dreamy blissful languor stealeth fast
Over my soul while musing peusively
On this fair vista steeped in rapt repose,
And I forget the busy throng of life
That it presents by day,—and almost now
I could imagine it some magic realm
Enchanted in far fairyland, beyond
The power of mortal reach.
                                But soon a voice
Says, " Supper's come at last, let's eat, and then
        to bed."

Waiting for the Dentist.

Though many dismal years I've been
 To dull old Care apprenticed,
Of smaller woes the worst I've seen
 Is—waiting for the dentist!

How dreary is the cheerless room
 Where pain must bide his pleasure,
The very chairs are steeped in gloom
 And seem to grieve at leisure,

As if his patients' molar grief,
 So uncontrolled its swelling,
For its fierce tide had sought relief
 By deluging the dwelling.

Books cannot soothe a rampant tooth
 Though they enrich a table,
Sorrow alone seems kin to truth,
 And joy a lying fable.

When from the window you, perchance,
  Behold sweet girlhood's graces,
They only make you look askance
  And think how sore your face is.

On many chairs and sofas, too,
  More martyrs round you languish,
You glance at them, they glance at you,
  And give a groan of anguish.

You deem it hard their turn arrives
  Before you in rotation,
Or they wax wrath that yours deprives
  Their case of consolation.

You muse upon the ruthless wrench
  That buys a tooth's departing,
Or how the stopping-pangs to quench,
  In which you may be starting;

Or haply on these ivory chips
  Harsh Nature may deny you,
But which the "golden key" equips
  Man's genius to supply you.

No words your mood of mind express,
  A mood devoid of quiet,

Where pain, delight, and keen distress
  Mingle in hopeless riot.

Yes, though much sorrow one must know
  While to old Care apprenticed,
The greatest unheroic woe
  Is—waiting for the dentist.

Notes.

Note to " At the Grave of Dante Gabriel Rossetti."

1. Rossetti died at Birchington-on-Sea, Kent, on the 9th of April, 1882.

Note to " Browning's Funeral—I."

2. See Browning's poem, entitled "In a Gondola."

Note to " The Taking of the Flag."

3. The epithet "Dutch rag" is said to have been the actual phrase used by the sailor whom Hopson addressed. The boy had only joined the fleet on the day before as a volunteer, and had previously been a tailor's apprentice. *Vide* "Sea Fights," p. 73. Professor Laughton, in "The Dictionary of National Biography," expresses his opinion, however, that the incident on which this poem is based has no historical foundation.

Notes to " The Keeping of the Vow."

4. When I first versified this incident, I was not aware that the subject had been already dealt with under the title of "The Heart of the Bruce," by Professor Aytoun.

5. It will be remembered that the struggle in Spain between the Moors and the Christians lasted for centuries.

6. It is evident, from what we know of his conduct, that Douglas regarded the war as pre-eminently a religious one.

Note to " The Death of Captain Hunt."

7. See "Battles of the British Navy," vol. i., p. 210.

Note to " João to Constança."

8. The *lesté* is a south-east wind felt in Madeira, and frequently prevalent for several days.   At the beginning or close of a *lesté* the sunrises and sunsets are superb. Purple is the colour particularly prominent.

Note to "Francisca to Jaspear."

9. The Portuguese guitar.

Note to " Lines on a Stone near the Summit of the Simplon Pass."

10. There was some desultory fighting in the Italian Alpine valleys before Napoleon the First's decisive victory of Marengo.

CHISWICK PRESS :—CHARLES WRITTINGHAM AND CO.
TOOKS COURT, CHANCERY LANE, LONDON.

CHARLES WHITEHEAD:
A FORGOTTEN GENIUS.

A MONOGRAPH

WITH EXTRACTS FROM WHITEHEAD'S WORKS.

BY MACKENZIE BELL.

New Edition.

With an Appreciation of Whitehead by
HALL CAINE.

CLOTH, 3*s.* 6*d.*

Times :—"It is strange how men with a true touch of genius in them can sink out of recognition ; and this occurs very rapidly sometimes, as in the case of Charles Whitehead. Several works by this writer ought not to be allowed to drop out of English literature, and a publisher might do worse than by reprinting some of them. They contain ever and again unquestionable evidence of power. Mr. Mackenzie Bell's sketch may consequently be welcomed for reviving the interest in Whitehead. . . . Whitehead's verse attracted the notice of two very different men, Dante Rossetti and Christopher North ; while one of his novels inspired a similar feeling in Dickens."

Contemporary Review :—"Mr. Mackenzie Bell has done a good service in introducing us to a man of true genius, whose works have sunk into mysteriously swift and complete oblivion. Judging by the extracts furnished by Mr. Mackenzie Bell, Charles Whitehead's poem, 'The Solitary,' and his novel, 'Richard Savage,' were both very remarkable works. . . . Mr. Mackenzie Bell writes in an excellent style, and his critical remarks are full of thoughtful good sense."

Athenæum :—"Whitehead was an interesting man, and produced some good work. He is deserving of resurrection."

Daily Chronicle :—"A kindly task has been executed with loving care in this critical monograph."

Daily News :—"This fascinating book. . . . Mr. Mackenzie Bell has done a peculiar service to letters."

Literary World :—"We cannot thank him too warmly for the labour he has bestowed in the cause of this remarkable man, whose enthusiastic but yet discerning champion he is. The critic who can see no faults in his favourites is as blind as love, but no accusations can be brought against Mr. Bell's critical acumen. He points with impartial finger to the glory and the flaw ; he gives extract after extract, both in prose and verse, with the accompaniment of a commentary which is always sane."

Morning Post :—"No fault can be found with the manner in which Mr. Mackenzie Bell has accomplished his difficult task. He has been inspired by an enthusiasm, which though some may feel it to be beyond the pathetic merits of the subject that creates it, is none the less honourable to the biographer's sense of justice and deep, far-reaching sympathy."

Globe :—"In rescuing Whitehead's memory from quasi-oblivion he has unquestionably done good service to literature. His monograph is carefully, neatly, and sympathetically built up. It contains (with the new preface and its appendix), all that is known about Whitehead's career and character, and furnishes an informing and readable estimate of his worth,—romancist, humorist, and what not."

Black and White :—"Mr. Bell's excellent monograph. This book deals with a fascinating man in a fascinating manner."

Public Opinion :—"As a critical introduction to the works of a man of genius, it could not be in better taste, or exhibit clearer judgment and a more discriminating sympathy."

Pall Mall Magazine :—"Mr. Mackenzie Bell's fascinating monograph."—*Mr. I. Zangwill.*

www.ingramcontent.com/pod-product-compliance
Lightning Source LLC
Chambersburg PA
CBHW020235030726
47497CB00009B/3103